First published 2007 by Walker Books Ltd
87 Vauxhall Walk, London SE11 5HJ

This edition published 2008

15 17 19 20 18 16 14

© 2007 Polly Dunbar

This book has been typeset in Windsor

Printed in China

British Library Cataloguing in Publication Data:
a catalogue record for this book is available
from the British Library

ISBN 978-1-4063-1246-1

www.walker.co.uk